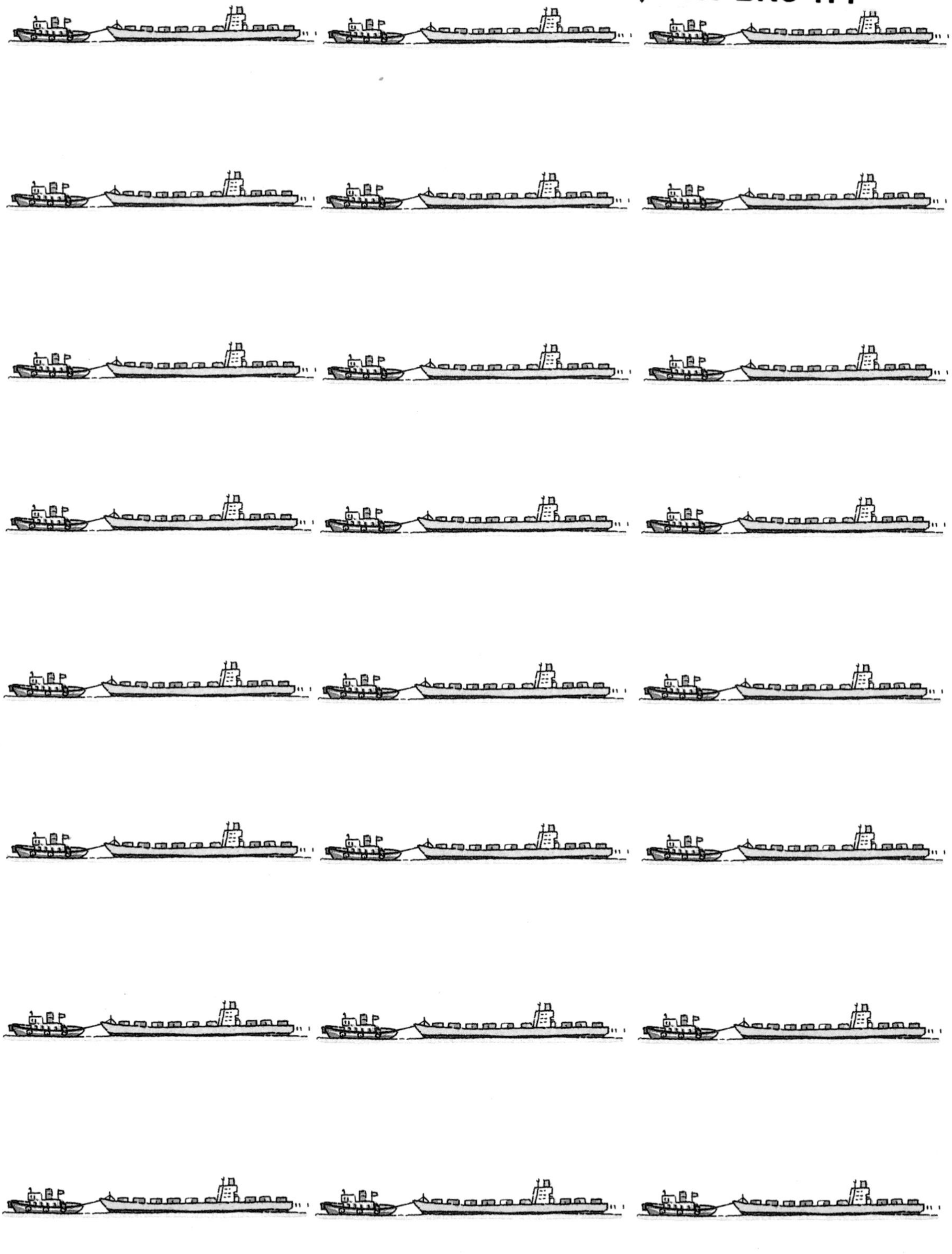

DK

A DORLING KINDERSLEY BOOK

Written by Angela Royston
Photography by Tim Ridley
Additional photography by Steve Shott (pages 10-11)
and Acorn Studios PLC, London (pages 16-17)
Illustrations by Jane Cradock-Watson and Dave Hopkins
Model makers Ted Taylor (pages 4-9, 14-15, and 18-21)
and Charles Somerville (pages 12-13)
Cruise ship model supplied by P&O Art and Memorabilia Collection
Container ship model supplied by P&O Containers Limited

Aladdin Books
Macmillan Publishing Company
866 Third Avenue
New York, NY 10022

Macmillan Publishing Company is part of the
Maxwell Communication Group of Companies.

Eye Openers ™

First published in Great Britain in 1992
by Dorling Kindersley Limited,
9 Henrietta Street, London WC2E 8PS

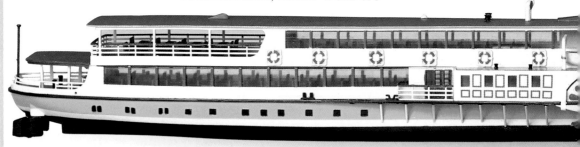

Reproduced by Colourscan, Singapore
Printed and bound in Italy by L.E.G.O., Vicenza

1 2 3 4 5 6 7 8 9 10

ISBN 0-689-71566-8

Library of Congress Catalog Card Number: 91-25687

·EYE·OPENERS·

Ships
and Boats

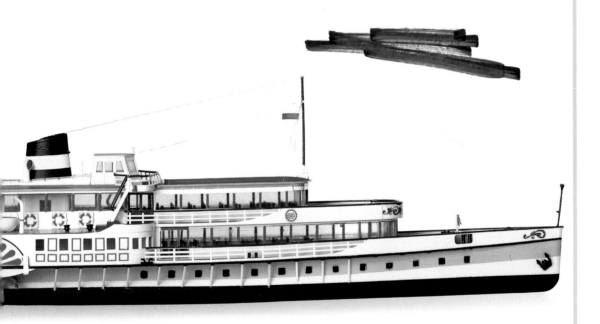

ALADDIN BOOKS
MACMILLAN PUBLISHING COMPANY
NEW YORK

Sailboat

A sailboat has giant sails.
Wind blows against the sails
and pushes the boat along.
The board under the back
of the boat is the rudder.
It is moved from side
to side and steers the
boat. Most people
sail for fun.

sails

rudder

keel

7

Motorboat

This motorboat has a powerful engine. It makes the propellers in the water turn very fast, which pushes the boat forward. A motorboat can slice through waves easily because of its long, narrow hull.

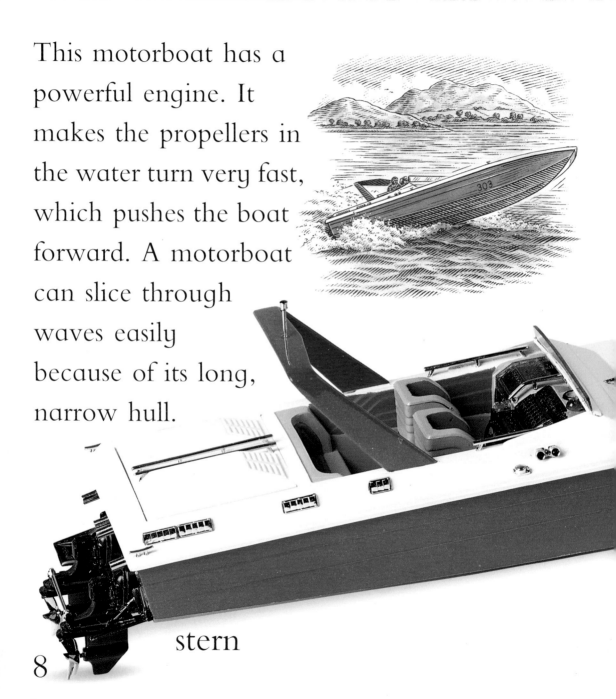

stern

8

propeller   engine   steering
                               wheel

bow

hull

303

Cruise ship

This cruise ship is like a floating hotel. It has a theater, stores, and swimming pools on board. People stay on board while the ship sails the seas. When the ship stops at a port, the people go ashore and visit different places.

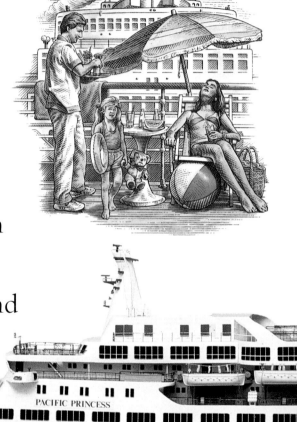

PACIFIC PRINCESS

PACIFIC PRINCESS

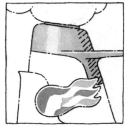

funnel

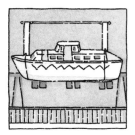

lifeboat

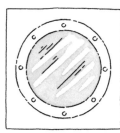

porthole

flag

Fishing boat

This fishing boat has a big net that catches fish. The net is pulled under water behind the boat. When the net is full, the fishermen use a winch to pull it onto the boat's deck. The fish are packed into boxes and taken to market.

SHEILA

INS 123

net

winch

INS 123

13

Frigate

A frigate is a warship. It has guns and missiles on board. A helicopter can land on a frigate's deck. The helicopters track down submarines. The captain uses computers to run the ship. The computers are in a room called the bridge.

F 209

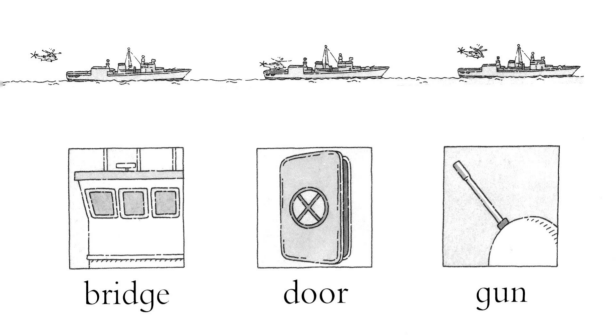

bridge

door

gun

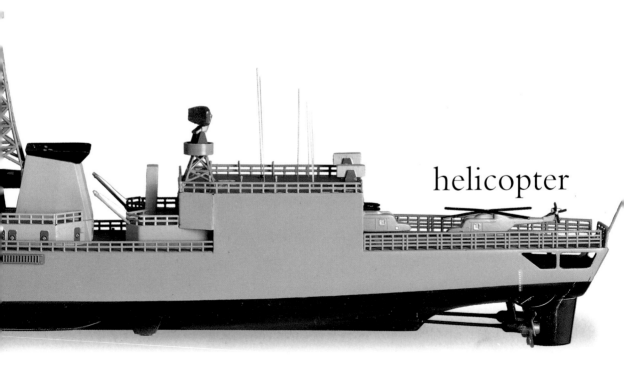

helicopter

Container ship

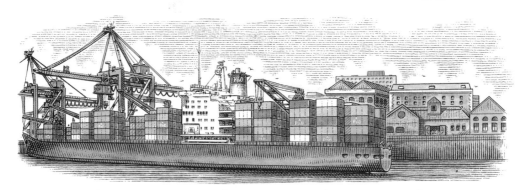

Container ships are huge. They carry cargo like clothes and cars. The cargo is packed into large steel containers. Tall cranes load and unload the containers at the docks.

lifeboat

funnel

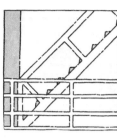
steps

containers

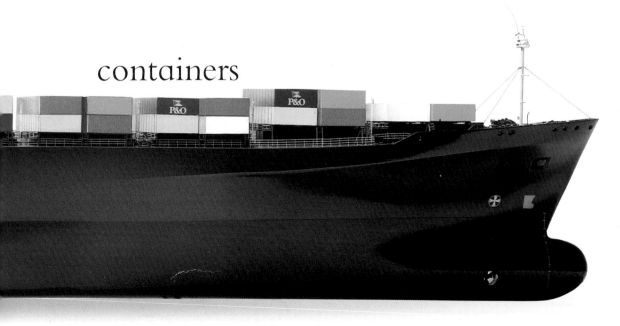

Tugboat

Tugboats are small, but they have powerful engines. They pull big ships, like ocean liners, in and out of harbors. Tugboats also rescue boats that have broken down. They pull these boats with thick, steel ropes.

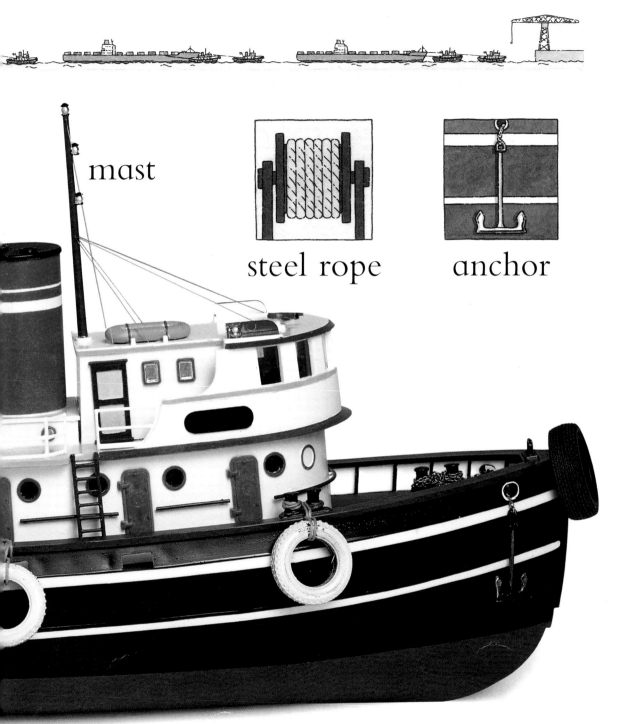

mast

steel rope

anchor

Paddleboat

This paddleboat was built many years ago. It traveled from town to town along a river. Steam moved the paddle wheels, pushing the boat forward. This paddleboat still takes people on rides for fun along the river.

GOETHE